5-MINUTE

ADA TWIST, SCIENTIST STORIES

BY GABRIELLE MEYER

Abrams Books for Young Readers

New York

Library of Congress Control Number 2021953190

ISBN 978-1-4197-6278-9

ADA TWIST ™/© Netflix. Used with permission.
Ada Twist, Scientist and the Questioneers created by Andrea Beaty and David Roberts
Book design by Charice Silverman

Printed and bound in China
10 9 8 7 6 5 4 3 2 1

Abrams Books for Young Readers are available at special discounts when purchased in quantity for premiums and promotions as well as fundraising or educational use. Special editions can also be created to specification. For details, contact specialsales@abramsbooks. com or the address below.

Abrams® is a registered trademark of Harry N. Abrams, Inc.

ABRAMS The Art of Books
195 Broadway, New York, NY 10007
abramsbooks.com

CONTENTS

Cake Twist 1

Twelve Angry Birds 15

The Banana Peel Problem ... 29

Movie Night 43

Mind Over Muscle 57

Garden Party 71

Bird's-Eye View 85

The Great Stink 99

Bend It Like Arthur 113

Rosie's Rockin' Pet 127

Ada Twist, Magicianist 141

Dadbot............................... 155

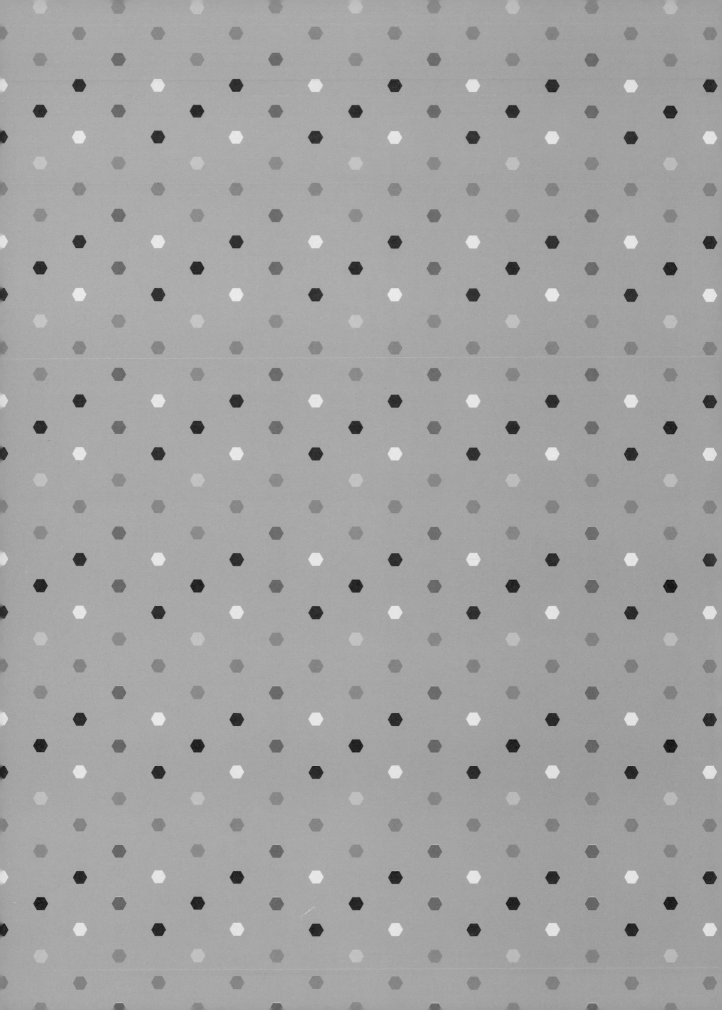

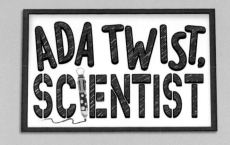

CAKE TWIST

Ada and Arthur notice that Dad is being extra lovey with Mom this morning. He even gives her the biggest smooch ever!

"Yuck!" Arthur groans. Ada giggles.

"Can't wait to see what you have planned for tonight, babe," Dad tells Mom before leaving for work.

Mom is confused. "Huh? What's tonight?"

Things get even stranger after that.

"Hey! The cereal has heart-shaped candy in it!" says Ada.

And someone drew lovey eyes on the eggs.

What is going on?

When Mooshu delivers Mom her favorite flowers, she finally realizes what's happening. Today is her anniversary with Dad, and she totally forgot!

Mom is so upset that she messes up the pancake on the stove. Ada calls the pancake a happy accident since it looks like a unicorn.

"Scientists make happy accidents all the time," she explains.

"That's lovely," says Mom. "But forgetting my anniversary is NOT a happy accident." What is she going to do? She didn't get Dad anything, and she has a big work project to finish, so she doesn't have time to go buy a gift.

Ada tells her mom not to worry. She'll find a way to help!

Iggy and Rosie come over to brainstorm, and Ada gets a great idea. They can bake her dad's famous Chocolate Surprise Cake! Ada doesn't know the exact recipe, but she's sure they can figure it out in the lab.

Baking *is* science, after all!

Ada remembers a little bit of the recipe from baking with her dad. She's pretty sure they need butter, baking soda, sugar, chocolate, eggs, and flour.

"And sprinkles on top, of course!" she adds.

They start baking, but when Ada pulls the cake out of the oven, she realizes there's a problem. The cake is ginormous!

"Uh-oh," she says. "Dad's cake is never this tall."

Rosie pokes the cake to see if it's done. It explodes, covering them in gooey chocolate!

"We must've put in too much baking soda," says Ada. "That made the cake way taller than it should be."

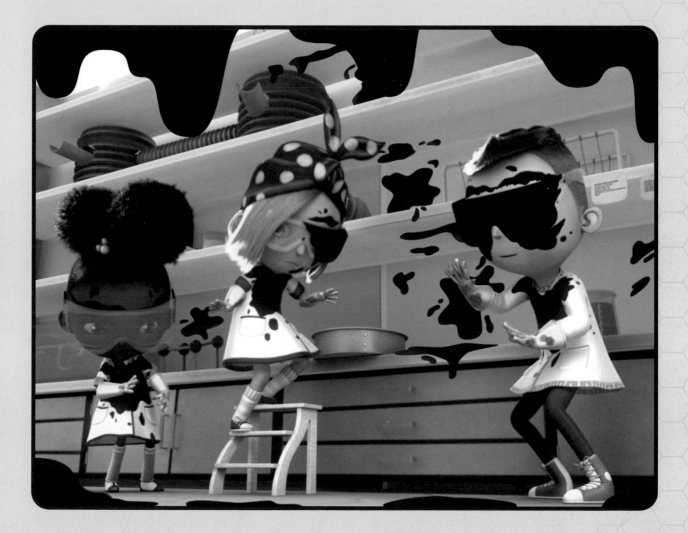

The little bakers try again, this time putting in way less baking soda. But when they take their new cake out of the oven, it deflates.

"Oh no, it sunk!" cries Ada.

"Just like our hopes and dreams," says Rosie with a dramatic sigh.

Rosie accidentally knocks over the baking soda, which spills onto a lemon. Ada observes the chemical reaction, and it inspires her to do some tests. When she puts a lot of baking soda on the lemon, it gets super bubbly and spills out over the plate. But when she puts just a little bit of baking soda on the lemon, it doesn't overflow!

"I forgot my dad's most important baking tip: Measure twice, bake once," says Ada. They just need to make sure all the measurements are exactly right!

They try baking the cake one more time, this time adding the perfect amount of baking soda. The cake looks just like Dad's Chocolate Surprise Cake! Hooray!

But when Ada tries it, she notices it's crunchy.

Wait a second . . . Dad's cake isn't usually this crunchy.

"Oh no!" cries Ada. "The sprinkles are supposed to be on the outside of the cake, not on the inside. This is a disaster!"

Ada apologizes to her mom for failing. "We didn't make Dad's Chocolate Surprise Cake."

"Maybe not," says Mom. "But you made *your* Chocolate Surprise Cake, with some surprise sprinkles inside. Sounds like a happy accident to me."

Ada realizes her mom is right. Hopefully her dad will like the cake, too!

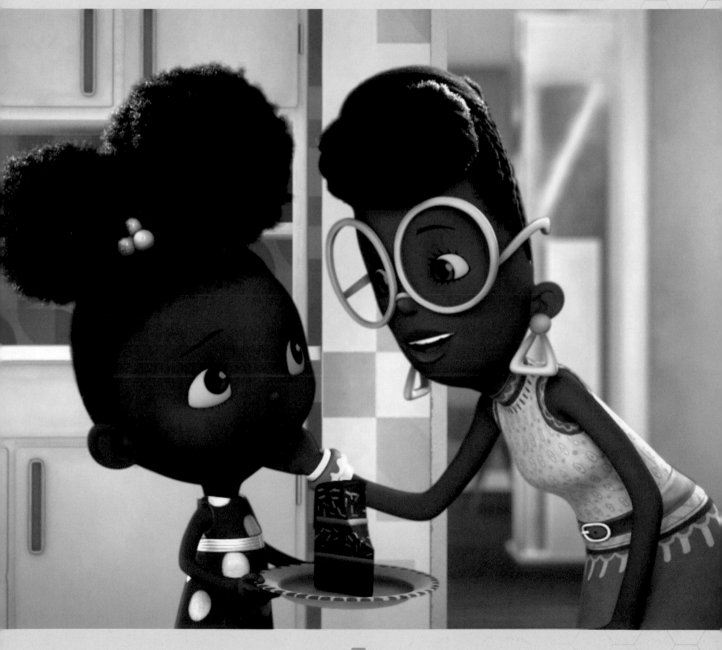

When Dad gets home, he takes a big bite of the cake.

"Hmm, this isn't my Chocolate Surprise Cake," he says. Ada starts to frown, but then Dad adds, "It's better! The crunchy sprinkles inside the cake are genius!" Ada's frown flips upside down!

"I'm glad you like it," she says. "I also added a secret ingredient: love."

TWELVE ANGRY BIRDS

It's hot, hot, hot today! Ada, Iggy, and Rosie are trying to cool off in the pool when suddenly, a bunch of birds start chirping loudly by the water feeder.

The kids take a closer look and notice the birds look angry.

"But why would all these cute birdies be angry?" asks Rosie.

"Here's a clue!" says Ada. "The water feeder is empty. They must be angry because they're thirsty."

Ada calls her mom outside so she can observe the birds.

"Wow," Mom says. "I don't think I've ever seen this many bickering birdies." She counts them. "There are twelve angry birds!" Mom doesn't understand why the water feeder is empty, though. Arthur filled it last night.

Ada ponders this. "Hmm. There has to be an explanation."

Just then, Mooshu jumps up to the water feeder.

"Oh no," Ada gasps. "Did Mooshu drink all the water that was meant for the birdies?"

Mom picks up the kitty. "Mooshu! You know what I said I'd do if you drank water from the feeder again." She carries Mooshu into the house.

"Wait, what is she going to do to Mooshu?" Ada asks, worried. "Oh no! Mom is going to give Mooshu away!"

They need to prove that Mooshu is innocent so Mom will let the kitty stay.

Ada, Iggy, and Rosie search for evidence about who or what might be behind the missing birdie water. They find an empty water bowl, a pawprint in the grass, and a furball. Now it's time to load the lab and examine their evidence!

But the evidence all points to Mooshu!

The pawprint from the scene of the crime is exactly the size of Mooshu's paw, and the fur is definitely kitty fur. Plus, Mooshu's water bowl was empty, which means she was probably thirsty. Maybe Mooshu did commit the crime after all.

"We still can't give up on Mooshu," says Ada. "If we're going to convince Mom not to give Mooshu away, we have to prove that she can be a good kitty."

The kids decide to hold a court case in the living room to defend the kitty. Ada calls Mooshu to the stand while Mom acts as the judge.

"Mooshu, isn't it true that while you've never been professionally trained, you can be very well behaved?" asks Ada.

Mooshu jumps off the chair and runs over to sit in front of the fan. Ada's worried. It's starting to look like Mooshu can't behave at all!

But then Ada notices that Mooshu looks very happy sitting in front of the fan. "Wait, Mooshu isn't a badly behaved kitty. She's just trying to cool off!" Ada exclaims.

"Makes sense," says Rosie. "It's really hot today."

This gives Ada an idea.

She thinks she knows what really happened to the water!

"Yes, it may be true that Mooshu was at the scene of the crime," Ada begins. "And she might not be the most well-behaved cat ever, but Mooshu didn't drink the birdie water. It disappeared through a scientific process called . . . evaporation!"

"Evaporation?" Iggy asks. "What's that?"

Ada explains that evaporation is when heat from the sun causes water to turn into a gas. It happens quickly on hot, dry days like today.

The case is closed! Mooshu is innocent!

"Now you won't have to give Mooshu away, Mom," says Ada.

Mom looks confused. "Give Mooshu away? I wasn't going to give her away. I was just going to give her a second bowl of water outside."

Ada, Iggy, and Rosie share a giggle. *Ohh,* that's what Mom meant.

They all go outside to add more water to the bird feeder. Now there are twelve very happy birds.

"And one happy kitty who gets to stay here forever," says Ada with a giggle.

THE BANANA PEEL PROBLEM

Ada, Iggy, and Rosie are playing at Rosie's apartment when they almost slip on a bunch of banana peels on the ground! Hmm, that's strange.

"Where are all these bananas coming from?" asks Iggy.

They follow the banana trail to the kitchen, where they find Rosie's mom struggling to peel a banana. "Ow!" she shouts.

Rosie grabs her mom's hands, concerned. "Oh no, Mom! What happened to your thumbs?"

"I'm fine, sweetie," she replies. "I just burned them while I was preheating the oven to make banana bread."

Banana bread? That must mean Great Aunt Rose is coming over! Rosie's Mom always bakes banana bread for Great Aunt Rose when she watches Rosie.

Rosie turns to her friends. "Guys, I know we had play plans, but I really want to help my mom."

Ada and Iggy want to help, too!

Rosie tells her mom to get ready for work.

The three scientists will solve the banana peel problem!

Instead of peeling all the bananas by hand, Rosie has a bigger idea.

"What if we find a way to help my mom peel lots of bananas not just today, but every day?"

Ada and Iggy love this plan. They'll invent a special contraption for peeling tons of bananas!

They build their contraption and show it to Rosie's mom.
"Presenting . . . the Banana-Rama!" says Rosie.

Her mom is impressed. "Wow! I thought you were in here peeling
bananas by hand," she says. "I should've known you three were
going to build a lean, mean peeling machine!"

Rosie turns on the Banana-Rama, but something goes wrong. The machine doesn't peel the bananas at all! Instead it just pokes a bunch of holes in them.

"Maybe the Banana-Rama just needs a little love tap to get it working," says Rosie.

She gives it a bump on the side, but it only makes things worse! The machine starts shooting bananas across the room! Ada, Iggy, and Rosie run for cover.

"We need to turn the machine off!" shouts Ada. She runs and slides across the kitchen floor, narrowly avoiding the flying bananas.

She makes it to the machine without getting hit and shuts it off. Phew!

"Wow. That was bananas!" says Rosie.

Rosie has another idea about how to fix the Banana-Rama. She removes the fork inside the machine and installs a pizza cutter instead. That's sure to work!

But when she tests it, the pizza cutter slices straight lines through the bananas instead of peeling them.

"Oh, phooey," says Rosie glumly. "I should just give up." Great Aunt Rose will be here soon, and they still haven't figured out how to make a contraption that peels bananas.

But Ada and Iggy won't let her give up yet. "We can still do it!" says a determined Ada.

Rosie thanks her friends for their support. Maybe she just needs to take another look at the bananas to solve the problem.

"Oh, doy! I know what our machine is missing!" exclaims Rosie.

"We need to add something to take the top off the bananas! That will help get the peeling started."

Rosie tinkers with the machine and adds a new piece to take the top off the bananas. They turn on the Banana-Rama and cross their fingers and their toes. Hopefully it works this time!

And it does! The bananas come out perfectly peeled.

Now that the Banana-Rama is a success and all the bananas are peeled, the kids help Rosie's mom finish baking the banana bread.

When Great Aunt Rose arrives, they all enjoy big, delicious slices of their banana bread.

Great Aunt Rose rubs her belly. "Mmm mmm mmm! That was some of the best banana bread I've ever had!"

Rosie's glad Great Aunt Rose liked it, because now they can make as much banana bread as they want with their lean, mean, banana-peeling machine!

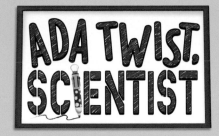

MOVIE NIGHT

Ada is so excited to host her first-ever movie night! She wants it to be absolutely perfect, so she picked a movie everyone will love, set out plenty of snacks, and even invented a machine that launches popcorn. "I call it the Popcorn Launcherette!" says Ada.

When she turns on the Popcorn Launcherette to demonstrate how it works, it malfunctions and starts shooting popcorn at Arthur!

"Ahh!" Arthur yells. "Shut it off!"

"Oopsies," Ada says with a giggle as she turns it off. "That's why an invention always needs lots of testing. Just ask Thomas Edison, the guy who invented the lightbulb. He tested almost ten thousand different ways to make a lightbulb before he found one that worked." The others are amazed. That's a lot of testing!

Movie night is about to start! Ada explains to the audience that she picked a movie using very precise calculations. It has the perfect mix of adventure, action, and romance.

She stands in front of the TV and says, "And now, it's time for our feature presentation, *Snuggle Warriors Three!*"

But just as she presses play on the remote, the power goes out!

"No, not tonight!" cries Ada. If there's no electricity, movie night will be ruined!

Mom and Dad leave to see if they can find the backup power generator in the garage.

Rosie gives everyone balloons to cheer them up. When she puts a balloon crown on Iggy's head, his hair gets all frizzy!

"Oops. Sorry, Iggy," Rosie says through laughter. "I forgot that balloons create static electricity."

"Wait . . . that's it! We can make our own electricity!" declares Ada.

"Thomas Edison found a way to do it, so we can too!"

First, they need to examine how electricity is made.

"Well, machines make electricity out of natural energy, like the sun or wind or rivers," says Ada. But that's a problem, because there's no wind or sun tonight.

"And I don't see any rivers," says Arthur.

Suddenly, Mooshu starts zipping around the room, chasing the beam from Ada's flashlight. They all giggle as they watch the cat pounce on the spotlight.

"Wow, Mooshu sure has a lot of energy," says Iggy.

This gives Ada an idea. "Maybe we can use Mooshu's energy to power the TV!" Yes! They'll make a special machine and call it the Mooshinator! Ada is relieved they have a plan. Once they make electricity, this night can go back to being perfect!

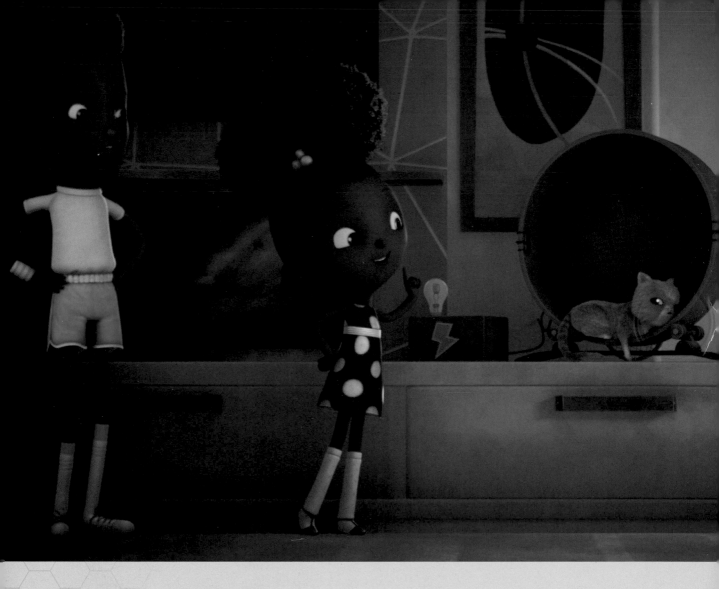

They place Mooshu in the Mooshinator, but the kitty just lies down in the wheel.

"No, Mooshu," says Ada. "For the machine to make electricity, you have to make the wheel spin by running."

But it looks like Mooshu would rather take a nap than run.

Ada slumps into the chair, upset.

"If we can't use the Mooshinator to make electricity, how are we going to watch *Snuggle Warriors Three*?" She lets out a big, sad sigh.

"This movie night is the opposite of perfect."

Dad and Mom come back from the garage. They have good news and bad news. The bad news is they didn't find the backup power generator, but the good news is that Dad found his old guitar!

"Come on, let's dance," says Dad as he plays a fun tune.

As they all dance around the living room, Ada realizes they're using tons of energy to boogie. The gears start turning in her brain, and she sneaks off to the lab.

In the lab, Ada makes calculations on her whiteboard. Maybe there's a way to turn dancing energy into electricity!

But no matter how hard she thinks, she can't seem to find a solution. And to make matters even worse, it's officially too late to start a movie. She trudges off to her room, defeated.

Ada's family and friends find her in her room.

"Why are you all by yourself, baby?" asks Mom. "Didn't you have fun dancing?"

"I did," responds Ada. "But I wanted to find a way to make electricity so movie night wouldn't be a failure."

Iggy is confused. "Failure? No way! Tonight was so much fun." Rosie and Arthur agree. It was the best movie night ever!

"Plus, you did discover several ways *not* to make electricity," adds Dad.

"Yeah," Arthur chimes in. "Just like Thomas Edison!"

Ada realizes they're right. The night was a scientific success after all!

Fortunately, it's not their bedtime yet. That means there's still time for more dancing!

Ada's first-ever movie night turned out even better than she could have hoped.

ADA TWIST, SCIENTIST

MIND OVER MUSCLE

Rosie went to her very first karate class today, and she can't wait to show Ada and Iggy her favorite moves: the Glitter Jab, the Unicorn Kick, and the Rainbow Roundhouse!

"Wow, that dojo seems like it was made for you, Rosie," says Ada.

But Rosie admits that she made those moves up. The real moves she learned in class weren't as exciting. Her karate teacher, Sensei Dave, thinks beginners should start with the basics.

"It's sooo boring," Rosie says. "I want to get to the fun parts and smash stuff, like Professor Flowerbomb!"

The kids ask Dad Twist if they can watch one of Professor Flowerbomb's videos online.

"Sure, sweets," says Dad. "Professor Flowerbomb is fierce!" They gather around Dad's computer to watch a whole video of Professor Flowerbomb smashing stuff.

"I have a PhD in POWER!" she yells, right before punching through a huge stack of bricks.

Dad is right—she *is* fierce!

They go to the backyard so Rosie can practice karate chopping through a wooden board.

"If Professor Flowerbomb can smash bricks, a tiny board should be a piece of cake," she says.

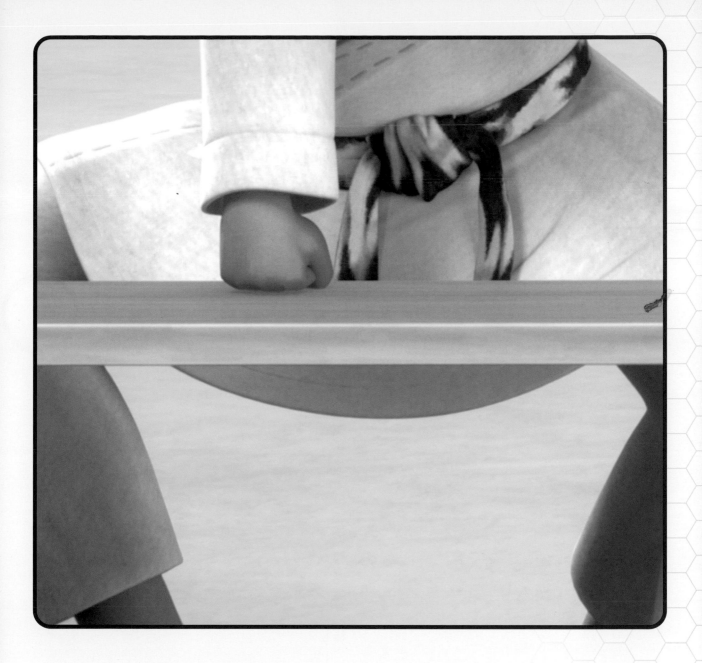

But when Rosie hits the board, it doesn't break.

"I don't get it," she says. "I powered up and flexed my muscles like Professor Flowerbomb, so why can't I smash it like she did?" Rosie thinks maybe it's because she's not as strong as Professor Flowerbomb. She just needs to get more muscles! Ada and Iggy say they'll help by working out with her.

They load the lab, which is now filled with gym equipment. "All right, let's get physical!" says Rosie. But when she tries jumping rope, she jumps up and down so quickly that she trips and falls.

"Maybe you need to go slower," suggests Ada.

"But I need to get muscles *fast*!" says Rosie.

Next, they try pushing sleds filled with toys, but no matter how hard Rosie pushes, her sled doesn't budge.

"Maybe try pushing with fewer toys," Iggy recommends.

"No way!" says Rosie. "Fewer toys equals fewer muscles."

After their long, failed workout, they return to the backyard.

"Phooey, my arms look exactly the same, and now they're all noodle-y," says Rosie. "I wanted to get muscles and do a karate chop, but this is a karate flop." She lets out a huge sigh. Maybe she should just give up.

But Ada and Iggy won't let that happen. "There's no quitting in karate," says Ada. "Or in science."

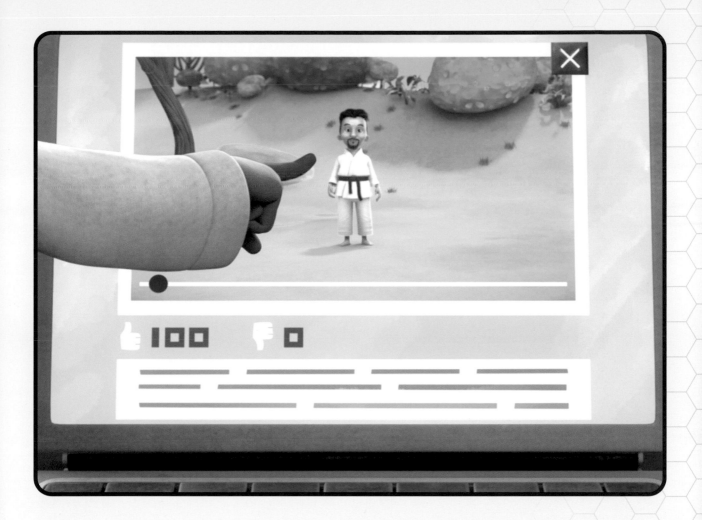

Iggy wonders if Rosie's karate teacher, Sensei Dave, has a video about breaking boards. Maybe he'll have some good tips!

But Rosie isn't so sure. "I don't know. Sensei Dave is a little guy. He probably can't smash stuff like Professor Flowerbomb."

"Well, let's check!" says Ada. They ask Dad Twist to search for a video featuring Sensei Dave, and he finds one!

Sensei Dave gives a mind-blowing lesson about breaking things using just your hands. "Being able to smash stuff is all about physics," he says. "It requires practice and precision. You need to use force and momentum focused on a small area."

He aims for the center of the bricks, where they are the weakest, then he winds up and hits. His hand smashes right through all the bricks!

They can't believe it! Sensei Dave's moves are incredible!

"So it's not all about strength and power after all," says Ada with excitement. "It's about physics!"

Now that Rosie has some great tips from Sensei Dave, she can't wait to try smashing the board again!

But even though Rosie uses Sensei Dave's tips, the board still doesn't break. This time, though, a small crack appears in the wood.

Ada and Iggy encourage Rosie. "Sensei Dave also said it takes practice. If you keep practicing, you'll be smashing through boards in no time!" says Ada.

Across the yard, Dad suddenly gasps. "No way! You kids might want to brace yourselves for this."

He shows them a video of Professor Flowerbomb's pile of bricks crumbling when she accidentally steps on them. Wait a second. Those aren't real bricks! They're made of foam!

"Wow. Professor Flowerbomb's power moves are power *fakes*," says Ada.

"Huh, I guess she needs to go back to the basics," says Rosie. "I'm definitely sticking with Sensei Dave."

Rosie leads them all through the basic karate exercises Sensei Dave taught her in class.

"I guess it is best to start from the beginning and take things slow," she says.

"Now, get ready to punch! Ki-ya!"

GARDEN PARTY

Ada and Rosie show up to Iggy's mom's house dressed for a garden party. They can't wait to spend the afternoon enjoying a picnic in the beautiful backyard!

There's just one problem: the garden isn't looking very beautiful today.

"Sweet zucchini!" exclaims Rosie when she sees the brown, wilted plants.

"I know," says Iggy. "I invited you over for a garden party, but this garden isn't exactly giving off a party vibe."

"Are these plants sad?" asks Ada.

"Or sleepy?" asks Rosie.

"No," says Iggy. "They're just not very healthy right now. My dad used to take care of them, but since he moved, he hasn't been able to."

Iggy's Mom brings the kids some scrumptious snacks. She tells them she's so sad her garden isn't healthy, but she just doesn't have time to take care of it.

"If only taking care of the plants was as easy as pressing a button," she says with a sigh.

"My mom might not have a green thumb, but she loves this garden," says Iggy. "I wish I could make it nice for her again."

"Iggy, we're scientists. And your friends," Ada says. "We'll help you!"

They study the sick plants in the garden and realize the ones in the shade of the umbrella are even droopier than the ones in the sun. Iggy also notices that the soil is very dry. That must mean the plants haven't gotten much water lately.

Ada has a hypothesis! "Plants must need sunlight and water to be healthy," she says. Now it's time to head to the lab to test the hypothesis!

In the lab, they give their test plant some sunshine, and it becomes greener!

Yes! They just proved the first part of their hypothesis:

Plants need sunshine to be healthy.

Next, they water the plant, and the leaves become less droopy!

"Woo-hoo! We proved part two of our hypothesis!" announces Ada. "Plants need water."

Back in the garden, they move the umbrella out of the way so all the plants get plenty of sun. Then they give the thirsty plants lots of water.

The plants are looking better, but it seems like they still need a little more love. Iggy calls his dad to ask for some expert gardening advice.

Iggy's dad tells them to add some fertilizer to the soil.

It's like vitamins for plants, so it will make them healthier!

Now that the plants have sun, water, and fertilizer, they look green and healthy again. They did it! But Iggy knows there's still one big issue.

"My mom can't do this much work in the garden every day," he says. "You heard her. She doesn't have the time."

"Hmm," Ada thinks. "We need to give your mom an easy way to take care of her garden."

"She did say she wishes she had a button to take care of the plants," says Rosie. So maybe they can build a machine that waters and fertilizes the plants with the touch of a button!

That's it! They get to work building a machine that automatically waters and fertilizes the plants, so Iggy's mom doesn't have to.

They present the Green Thumbinator machine to Iggy's mom.

"Wow. Now *that* I have time for," she says. "Thanks to you three, I finally have a green thumb. And a green garden."

After all their hard work, they sit in the beautiful backyard and enjoy strawberry smoothies that Iggy's mom made with fresh strawberries from the garden.

"This is the best garden party I've ever been to," says Ada.

Iggy and Rosie agree!

BIRD'S-EYE VIEW

Ada, Iggy, and Rosie are birdwatching in the Twists' backyard. They're even wearing bird costumes, so they won't scare the birdies.

Through their binoculars, they spot a mama bird and baby bird in a nest. Ada and Rosie think the teeny birdie is the cutest thing they've ever seen, but Iggy isn't so sure.

"Birds kind of freak me out," he admits.

The mama bird flies off. "She must be getting food for the baby," says Rosie.

Suddenly, a big gust of wind blows the nest out of the tree. Rosie runs and catches the baby bird, but nobody catches the nest in time. It smashes into the ground and breaks!

Oh no! The birds' home is ruined.

Ada decides they need to make the baby bird a new nest so he stays safe until his mama comes back.

Even though birds freak Iggy out, he still wants the baby birdie to be safe. Plus, he always loves a design challenge.

"I'll design the coolest, most creative nest ever!" he says.

They head to the lab and examine the broken nest.

"Wow. Birds are really good architects," he says.

Based on the design of the old nest, it looks like their new nest will need twigs, leaves, and fluff. Iggy gets to work on his design.

Iggy is so proud of his cool nest design! It looks awesome!

But first they need to put a test bird in the nest to make sure it's safe for the real baby bird. Rosie makes a balloon owl, but when she puts it in the nest, it pops! Uh-oh. This nest is way too pokey and sharp for the baby bird. Good thing they tested it first.

Next, Iggy designs a soft, fluffy nest out of leaves and feathers, but it blows away in the wind.

It was *too* soft and fluffy!

Iggy says maybe he should just give up.

"I wanted to design a cool, creative nest for you," Iggy tells the baby bird. "But I guess I'm not as good of an architect as a bird."

Ada and Rosie tell him he can't give up yet. They need to make a nest so the baby bird has a safe home!

"I just wish there was a way to know what kind of nest the bird would want," says Iggy.

This gives Ada an idea!

They should build a gigantic nest so they can see things from the bird's point of view.

They test out their human-sized nest and make sure that it's strong but not pokey, and soft but not too soft. They decide that the design is perfect!

"Thanks for not letting me give up," Iggy tells Ada and Rosie.

They give him a big hug. That's what besties are for! Now they just need to make the nest bird-sized.

"I hope Kiwi likes his new home," says Iggy when they finish building the nest.

"Who's Kiwi?" asks Ada.

Iggy explains that he named the baby bird Kiwi, since it looks like a little kiwi fruit. Kiwi hops around inside the nest and chirps happily. He loves it!

"We did it!" exclaims Iggy. "We just had to look at the nest from the bird's point of view."

Ada writes down a new theory in her notebook, the Bird's-Eye View Theory: Sometimes you can solve a problem by looking at it from another point of view.

After Ada's dad puts the nest high up in the tree, the mama bird returns home.

It looks like she loves her new nest!

"So, do you like birds now, Iggy?" Ada asks.

He shrugs. "I don't know about birds, but I definitely love Kiwi."

THE GREAT STINK

Ada, Iggy, and Rosie are playing their favorite board game, Goblins and Dragons, when a super stinky smell fills the room.

"That smell is terrible!" Ada exclaims. "We have to find out what it is!"

They sniff their way to the kitchen, but the only smell in here is a delicious one coming from Dad's veggie soup. Dad explains that he used the same veggies in the salad, too.

"I have an interesting observation," says Ada.

"The veggies in the soup smell really good, but the veggies in the salad barely smell at all."

The three kids are sniffing the salad veggies when suddenly, they smell the stink again! Yes!

"Come on!" says Ada. "Let's follow our noses and find that stink!"

They sniff all over the house, trying to figure out where the stinky smell is coming from.

"Aha!" shouts Ada. "We've found the source of the Great Stink: Arthur's tennis shoes!"

Yuck. His shoes are super smelly!

Arthur appears behind them. "Uh, what are you kids doing?"

"We made a fascinating discovery," Ada tells him. "You have stinky shoes!"

Arthur sighs. "I know. I don't want them to stink up the whole house, though. I've tried everything to get rid of the smell, but de-stinking my shoes is impossible."

Ada, Iggy, and Rosie say they can help him solve his stinky shoe problem with science!

The three little scientists head to the lab to do some tests. Since they don't want to ruin Arthur's shoes, they'll experiment on a stinky test shoe. They make sure to plug their noses, so they don't have to smell the stinkiness the whole time.

They test out *a lot* of de-stinking sprays on the shoe, but nothing makes it less smelly. One of their experiments even melts the shoe into goo!

"Maybe Arthur is right," Ada says. "De-stinking his shoes is impossible."

Suddenly, Rosie's stomach growls. "Oopsies." She giggles. "I just can't wait for dinner. Your dad's soup smells so good, Ada!"

Ada agrees, but she still doesn't know why the soup smells better than the salad, even though they both have the same veggies.

"I don't know either," says Rosie. "But I do know that soup makes my belly feel happy and warm."

This gives Ada an idea! "I have a hypothesis! Maybe hot things smell stronger than cold things."

To test their hypothesis, they turn up the temperature in the lab so it's super hot. When they take off their nose plugs to sniff Arthur's tennis shoes, they all yell, "Ewwww!"

"It's the smelliest smell I've ever smelled," groans Iggy.

"And the stinkiest stink I've ever stunk!" says Rosie.

Next, they turn down the temperature to make the lab super cold. They unplug their noses and take a big whiff.

"It smells like . . . nothing!" says Rosie.

That means they proved their hypothesis! Things smell stronger in hotter temperatures than they do in colder temperatures. Now they know how to stop Arthur's shoes from stinking up the house!

Iggy designs an ice palace using a shoebox to keep Arthur's shoes nice and cold. Ada and Rosie help build it.

Arthur walks in and sees Ada putting his shoes in the ice palace shoebox.

"Hey, what are you doing to my shoes?" he asks.

"We're freezing the stink!" Ada explains. "The cold air keeps the stink from going all over the place."

He sniffs. "Wait, you're right. I don't smell anything! You know, you kids might be onto something with this science stuff."

Later at dinner, they all enjoy Dad's delicious veggie soup and salad.

"This soup tastes just as good as it smells, Mr. T," says Rosie.

"Yeah," agrees Arthur. "And I'm really glad this soup is the *only* thing smelling up the house."

BEND IT LIKE ARTHUR

The Twists are gathering old items to donate for the school fundraiser. Ada is donating her old lab goggles, and Dad is donating tons of his old T-shirts.

Arthur comes running out of the house.

"Wait! I have one more thing to give away: a barely used soccer ball! No dents, fully inflated, and in mint condition."

Mom and Dad pass the ball back and forth like soccer pros. The kids are impressed with their skills!

"Little man, why are you giving this away?" asks Dad.

Arthur shrugs. "Soccer's not really my thing."

"Why isn't it your thing?" asks Ada.

Arthur sighs. "I stink at it, okay? I've never even scored a goal."

Ada finds this strange. Arthur is great at sports, so it doesn't make sense that he's bad at soccer. She gets an idea.

"We can help you score a goal . . . with science! Science and sports go great together!"

Ada says that first they need to observe his kick.

But when Arthur winds up and tries to kick the ball, he loses his balance and falls!

"See? I'm not good at soccer!" he groans.

Ada has a hypothesis: "If you learn how to kick, you'll be able to score a goal."

Ada, Iggy, and Rosie brainstorm ways to make Arthur a better kicker. Ada thinks they should make him a bionic kicking leg that will help him learn to kick like a pro!

The little sports scientists build the device in the lab, then show it to Arthur.

"Presenting . . . the Kicker!" says Iggy.

"Put it on, Arthur," encourages Ada. "This should give you the perfect kick!"

But it doesn't give him the perfect kick. He tries again and again, but the soccer ball still doesn't come close to going in the goal.

"This is hopeless," says Arthur. "I should just give up."

Ada, Iggy, and Rosie encourage him not to give up, but he's made up his mind.

"I'm going to stick with something I'm already good at, like tennis," he says. "It's more fun."

"I don't get it," says Rosie as they all watch Arthur hit the tennis ball against the side of the house. "He's so good at tennis. Why isn't he good at soccer?"

"Yeah," agrees Iggy. "Arthur is great at tennis. He practices it all the time."

Wait, that's it! "I think I just connected the polka dots!" says Ada. "Arthur is good at tennis because he *practices*." She has a new hypothesis: If Arthur wants to score a goal, he needs to practice.

Arthur agrees to run some soccer drills in the backyard. Mom and Dad come out to cheer him on, and Mom quickly notices a problem with his kicking technique.

"You need to kick with the inside of your foot," she says. "Not with the tips of your toes."

Arthur tries kicking with the inside of his foot, and this time the ball soars through the air . . . and into the net!

GOOOOOAL!

He did it! He scored his first-ever goal!

It turns out that practice really does help.

Ada, Iggy, and Rosie are thrilled for Arthur! They run and pile on top of him.

"Thanks for not giving up on me, Lil A," says Arthur.

Ada gives her brother a gigantic hug. "You're welcome, Big A. Turns out science and sports are great teammates, just like us!"

ROSIE'S ROCKIN' PET

Ada, Iggy, and Rosie are testing out a brand-new kitty toy that Ada designed for Mooshu. They conclude that Mooshu loves it!

"Mooshu is so cute!" says Rosie. "I wish I had a pet. But since my mom travels for work, she said we wouldn't be able to have one." "I guess that makes sense," says Ada. "Taking care of a pet is a lot of work."

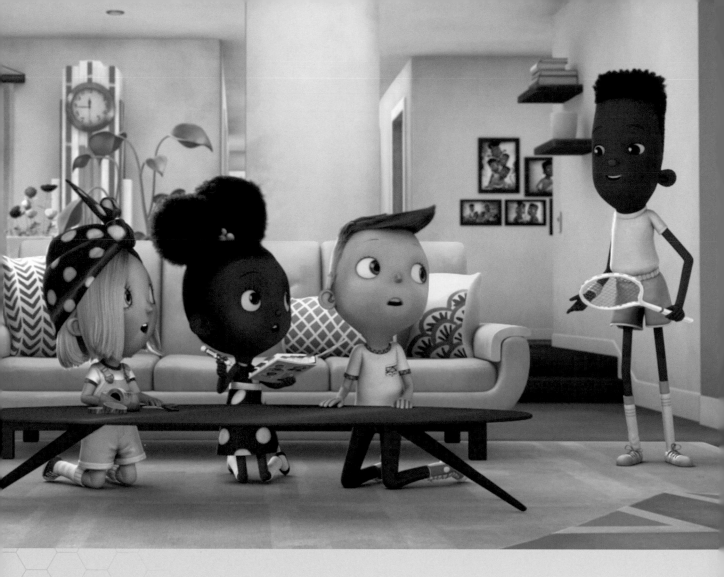

Rosie agrees. She could only have a pet that doesn't need to eat, play, or snuggle.

"Sounds like a rock," Arthur says as he walks into the room.

Wait, that's it! Rosie jumps up with excitement. "Yeah! I can get a pet rock!"

"Um, I was kidding," says Arthur.

But Rosie isn't kidding. She's going to get her very first pet today.

"We've got to go to the park to find my rock!" she says.

Ada goes into her mom's office to see if she can take them to the park.

"I'd love to!" Mom says. "I'm stuck on a work problem, and when that happens, taking a brain break usually does the trick."

At the park, the three friends gather a ton of rocks for Rosie.

"That's a pretty big pile of possible pets," says Iggy.

"Yeah," agrees Ada. "How are you going to choose which one to take home, Rosie?"

"I could never choose just one!" Rosie says. "There's something special about each rock." She wants to take them ALL home.

Ada surveys the giant pile of rocks. "Hmm. How are we going to get that many rocks home?"

"Easy-peasy," says Rosie. "We'll put them in our pockets!"

But carrying that many rocks in their pockets is NOT easy. The rocks are so heavy it makes it hard for them to walk. There's no way they'll make it all the way home!

They need to come up with a creative way to get the rocks back home, but they can't think of a single good idea in their brainstorm.

"Oh no!" cries Ada. "I think we ran out of ideas! My mind feels like goo."

"And my mushy feels mind," says Iggy. "Oops. I mean my mind feels mushy."

Just then, Ada sees her mom waving at them from across the park. This gives her an idea!

"I think I just connected the polka dots! When my mom is stuck on a work problem, she says taking a brain break usually helps." Maybe they just need to give their brains some time off. "I think it's time for a play break!"

Ada, Rosie, and Iggy play all over the park. They play hide-and-seek, take turns on the seesaw, and smell tons of sunflowers.

Finally, their brains don't feel mushy or gooey anymore!

Now that their brains are working again, they get back to brainstorming.

"I've got it!" says Rosie. "We can build a cart with wheels so we can pull the rocks home."

It's the perfect idea! And they can call their contraption the Rosie Rock Hauler!

They fill the Rosie Rock Hauler with all of Rosie's new rock pets, then wheel it back home. Success!

When Rosie's mom comes to pick her up later that day, Rosie introduces her to all her new pets.

"I never thought we'd be able to have a pet with my travel schedule," says Rosie's mom. "But we can definitely take care of pet rocks. What a creative idea!"

Rosie loves each of her new pet rocks, but she really wants to give one to both Ada and Iggy.

Now they all have pet rocks!

Mooshu looks up at Ada and lets out a worried *meowww.*

Ada giggles. "Don't worry, Mooshu. I may have a pet rock now, but you're still my favorite kitty."

ADA TWIST, MAGICIANIST

At dinner, Dad Twist asks the kids if they want to learn the secret to a really good burp.

"Yes, please!" they all shout.

Dad takes a big gulp of fizzy soda water then lets out a humongous burp! Ada, Iggy, and Rosie can't stop laughing!

"Thank you, thank you," says Dad. "The carbon dioxide in fizzy drinks causes burps. Cool, huh?"

"Carbon dioxide?" Ada taps her pen to her chin as she thinks. "Where have I heard of that before?" She flips through her notebook. "Oh, here it is," she says.

"We breathe in oxygen, then our bodies turn that into a chemical compound called carbon dioxide, which we breathe out!"

Suddenly, the lights turn off in the kitchen and Arthur's voice booms throughout the room. "Presenting . . . the one, the only, the amazing . . . Arthur-cadabra!"

Arthur jumps into the room wearing his magician's hat and cape. Everyone applauds. That was a very dramatic entrance!

"For tonight's magic trick, I'm going to make this bottle of ink disappear!"

Everyone *ooooooohs*. They can't wait to see Arthur's trick.

Arthur bobbles the ink bottle in his hands and drops it, spilling dark ink all over the white tablecloth. Oh no! What a mess!

But then Arthur waves his hands and blows on the tablecloth, and the ink stain disappears. Wow. It really is like magic!

Everyone claps for Arthur-cadabra. What an incredible trick!

"How'd you do that, Arthur?" asks Ada.

"Sorry, Lil A. Can't tell you," he says. "A magician never reveals their secrets."

But Ada is always on the hunt for answers to her questions, and this is one mystery she needs to solve.

The next morning, she calls Rosie and Iggy over for an emergency brainstorm.

"I have to know how Arthur did his trick!" she declares.

"There's only one explanation," says Rosie. "Your brother is a wizard."

But that doesn't seem right to Ada. She's known Arthur a long time, and she's pretty sure he's not a wizard.

"Maybe he used something to clean up the ink really fast without us seeing it," says Ada. "Let's go to the lab and test out some ways to get ink out of fabric."

In the lab, they test out ways to clean up ink stains using solutions like lemon juice, dish soap, and vinegar. But nothing gets the ink out!

"Ugh! Nothing is working!" Rosie pounds her fist on the workstation in frustration. The shelves begin to wobble, then jars of vinegar and baking soda fall off the shelf and into the model volcano.

Uh-oh. Vinegar and baking soda? That's how you make a . . . VOLCANIC ERUPTION!

Suddenly, the volcano erupts with bubbly lava. "RUN!" yells Ada.

They run as fast as they can away from the lava. Ada and Rosie leap up onto the desk, but Iggy trips and falls!

"Leave me," he says. "Save yourselves!"

But Ada and Rosie would never leave a friend behind. They grab Iggy's hand and pull him to safety just in time!

"Whoa. That was a major chemical reaction!" says Ada. This gives her an idea. "Hey, what if Arthur's magic trick was a chemical reaction?"

"Interesting theory," says Rosie. "But Arthur didn't mix the ink with anything else."

Wait . . . yes, he did! "He breathed on it, remember?" says Ada. "And what chemical compound do we breathe out?" Carbon dioxide! He must have used a special ink that disappears when mixed with carbon dioxide. Ada solved Arthur's trick!

That night at dinner, Ada can't wait to tell Arthur she figured out his trick. But Arthur isn't as excited. He gets up from the table and stomps out of the room.

Ada is confused. "What's wrong with Arthur?"

"I think he feels like you ruined his trick, baby," explains Mom. "Arthur doesn't do his magic tricks so we can solve them. He does them to entertain us." Oh boy. Ada feels like she really messed up.

Ada wants to make a super special apology for Arthur, so she writes him a letter with invisible ink. To read the letter, he has to put it under a hot lamp then wait for the ink to slowly appear. It's the magic of chemistry!

Arthur accepts Ada's apology. "Hey, want me to teach you a magic trick?" he asks. Ada would LOVE that!

The next night, Arthur-cadabra and Ada Twist Magicianist put on a special magic show for their parents, Iggy, and Rosie.

Ada magically pulls a coin out from behind Iggy's ear, and Iggy is blown away. "Whoa! How'd you do that?" he asks.

"Sorry," Ada says as she winks at her brother. "A magician never reveals their secrets."

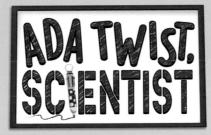

DADBOT

Ada, Iggy, and Rosie are using a powerful electromagnet to search for cool magnetic things in the garage when they come across a hunk of metal in the corner.

"Whoa, what is that?" asks Iggy.

"A project my mom started a long time ago," explains Ada. "I wonder why she never finished it."

When they go back inside, they find Mom trying to cook, clean, do laundry, and take a phone call at the same time.

"That's why she hasn't finished her project!" Ada realizes. "My mom is too busy, especially since my dad is at a book conference this weekend." The kids decide they need to find a way to help her out, and Ada has just the idea! They head to the lab and get to work.

The next morning, Mom comes into the kitchen and runs right into . . . a robot! She screams!

Ada skips into the room. "Oh good," she says happily. "You've met Dadbot! I built this robot to help you around the house so you can finish your project in the garage."

Even though Mom is a little weirded out by Dadbot, she is touched that Ada wanted to help her. "Thanks, baby. Sometimes I need to admit I can't do everything." She can't believe she gets to spend the whole day working on her special project!

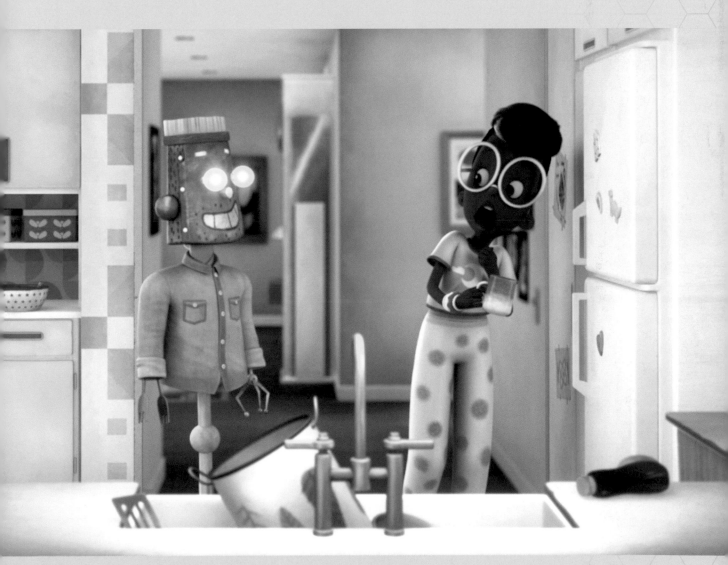

Arthur, Iggy, and Rosie are amazed that Ada taught a robot how to clean and cook.

"Dadbot has artificial intelligence," explains Ada. "That's how machines think and learn."

"Can you teach him to do other stuff, like serve tennis balls?" asks Arthur.

Ada shrugs. "Sure. Let's try it!"

Ada programs Dadbot to serve tennis balls to Arthur, and it works!

"Wow. That was incredible!" says Arthur. "Let's teach him to do more stuff!"

Ada flips open his control panel and starts typing in code as the others throw out ideas.

"Program him to breakdance!" says Arthur.

"Oooh, and to tell knock-knock jokes," suggests Rosie.

"And protect us from scary intruders!" adds Iggy.

Ada keeps typing in one suggestion after another. Finally, she says that's enough. Her fingers need a break!

But when Ada turns Dadbot back on, the bot malfunctions and starts chasing Mooshu all over the house, knocking lamps and plants over as he goes. Uh-oh! They tried to program Dadbot to do too many things, and now his system is overloaded!

"We should get Mom!" says Arthur.

Ada shakes her head. "No! I wanted Dadbot to make Mom's life easier, not harder. We've got to fix this without her."

There's only one way to stop the out-of-control bot. They have to catch him and press his reset button!

The kids set traps for Dadbot all over the house, but he gets away every time.

Ada feels like she messed up big time.

"We're never going to get close enough to Dadbot to reset him. Why'd I have to make him so fast?"

The kids all collapse in the living room, exhausted. The house is a total disaster, and they still don't know how to catch Dadbot.

"Uh-oh. Mom alert!" warns Arthur. "She's coming inside!"

When Mom sees the messy house, she gasps. "What happened in here?!"

Ada admits to her mom that she failed. "I programmed Dadbot to do too many things. I'm sorry, Mom."

Mom gives Ada a comforting hug. "We all try to do too much sometimes," she says. "I would know."

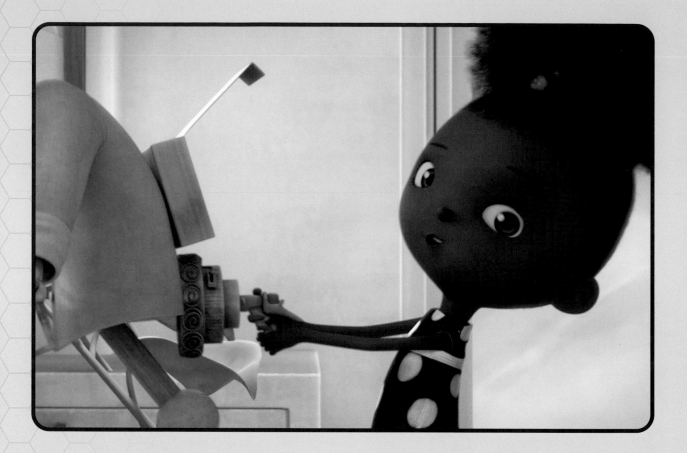

Mom has an idea, though. "Instead of chasing Dadbot, is there a way to bring him to us?"

Ada lights up.

"Yes, there is! Mom, you're a genius!"

Ada uses her powerful electromagnet to pull Dadbot to them. "Sorry Dadbot, but it turns out that trying to do too many things at the same time isn't a good idea," she says, then presses Dadbot's reset button. Phew! They finally got the wild bot under control!

When the real Dad comes home, he's surprised to find Ada and Arthur cleaning up the house.

"We're going to help out more so Mom's system doesn't get overwhelmed like Dadbot's did," Ada explains.

Dad scratches his head, confused. "Dadbot?"

Ada introduces Dad to Dadbot. "I programmed him to do just one thing: sweep!"

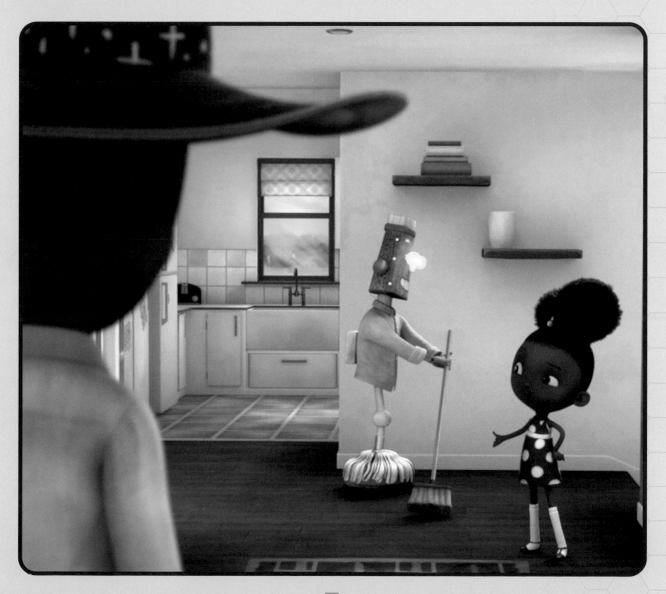

Mom calls her family outside. She finally finished her project! Ada, Arthur, and Dad are amazed when they see the four-person bike that Mom built all by herself.

"I wanted to make something we could all enjoy together," she says. "Now, come on. Let's ride!"

The four Twists hop on the bike and ride off down the street. Dadbot waves goodbye to them as he sweeps the front porch.

CHECK OUT THESE OTHER BOOKS STARRING

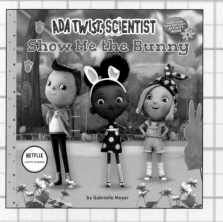

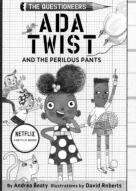

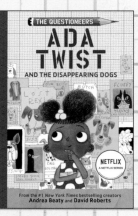

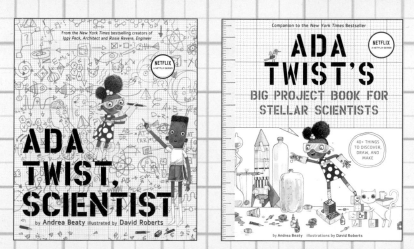

There's more to discover at **Questioneers.com**.